MY MADDY

To Amy, aka "Maddy"—GP

Thinking of you, Olivia and Caleb.—VT

Magination Press is a registered trademark of the American Psychological Association. Order books here: www.apa.org/pubs/magination, or call 1-800-374-2721.

Book design by Susan White and Rachel Ross
Printed by Sonic Media Solutions, Medford, NY

Library of Congress Cataloging-in-Publication Data
Names: Pitman, Gayle E., author. | Tobacco, Violet, illustrator.
Title: My Maddy / by Gayle E. Pitman ; illustrated by Violet Tobacco.
Description: Washington, DC : Magination Press, [2020] | "American Psychological Association." | Summary: A child celebrates her Maddy, who is neither mommy nor daddy but a little bit of both, like so many things in nature. Includes note to parents.
Identifiers: LCCN 2018038334 | ISBN 9781433830440 (hardcover) | ISBN 1433830442 (hardcover)
Subjects: CYAC: Parent and child—Fiction. | Gender identity—Fiction.
Classification: LCC PZ7.P648 My 2020 | DDC [E]—dc23
LC record available at https://lccn.loc.gov/2018038334

Manufactured in the United States of America
10 9 8 7 6 5 4 3 2 1

My Maddy

by Gayle E. Pitman, PhD

illustrated by Violet Tobacco

MAGINATION PRESS • WASHINGTON, DC
American Psychological Association

Most mommies are girls.
Most daddies are boys.
But lots of parents are
neither a boy nor a girl.
Like my Maddy.

Sometimes my Maddy's eyes look green, and sometimes they look brown.

Sometimes they look like both, or something completely different.

"Why is that?"
I ask Maddy.

"They're hazel," Maddy says. "It's a beautiful color all its own."

Maddy's hair flows from sort of brown, to sort of blonde, to kind of both, but not really either.

If only there were a word like "hazel" for hair.

Maddy wakes up at the crack of dawn,
way before I get up.

"I like watching the sunrise," Maddy tells me.
"It's not day and it's not night.

It's something in between, and kind of both,
and something all its own.

The sky changes from red, to pink, to yellow."

Every morning, Maddy drinks coffee while eating breakfast with a spork.

"I love sporks," says Maddy.

"It's not a spoon or a fork, but kind of both. That way, you only need one utensil."

Every day, Maddy walks me to and from school.
We talk about all kinds of things.

"What's your favorite time of the year, Maddy?"

"Fall and spring," says Maddy.

"The leaves turn colors in the fall," I say.
"And in the spring, flowers bloom."

"Yes," says Maddy. "Things change in fall and spring."

Before Maddy leaves, I get a big kiss.

Maddy's kisses feel like sandpaper
against my face.

While I'm in school, Maddy rides a motorcycle to work every day.

"It's not a car or a bicycle. It's kind of both, and it's something all its own," Maddy always says.

Maybe someday Maddy will take me for a ride on it.

When Maddy picks me up from school, I get a big bear hug.

Now I know how baby bears feel!

One day, on our way home, it started to drizzle. The sun shone through the raindrops.

"Look!" I pointed towards the sky.
"A rainbow!"

"The most beautiful things happen between the rain and the sun, don't they?" said Maddy.

When I get home,
it's after lunch
but before dinner.

I'm usually
starving by then.

Maddy fixes me a snack
to tide me over.

After dinner, before bedtime,
Maddy reads stories to me.

They're about imaginary things,
but Maddy makes them feel real.

Every night, Maddy tucks me in.

"Good night, my sweet child,"
says Maddy.

"Good night, Maddy.
I love you."

"I love you too. Sleep well,
and have magical dreams."

And between the time
I fall asleep and the time
I wake up, I do.

Some of the best things in the world are not one thing or the other, but in between, and kind of both, and something entirely fantastically their own.

Like my MADDY.

Note to Readers

"Most mommies are girls. Most daddies are boys. But a lot of parents are neither a boy nor a girl. Like my Maddy."

As the story shows us, a Maddy is a parent who is in some ways like a blend of a Mommy and a Daddy, and is also a unique kind of parent, just as the word "Maddy" blends the words "Mommy" and "Daddy" to make a new word. Maddy is used in some families to describe a parent who is transgender or gender diverse. (For the purpose of this Note, I will refer to transgender and gender diverse people as "trans," even though not all transgender and gender diverse people identify with the term "trans.") Other common terms that may be used to describe parents who are trans include "Baba" and "Mapa." This story's Maddy apparently has a gender identity that is not male or female but something that is "a bit of both and something all its own." Gender identities like this are often referred to as "non-binary" in that they are gender identities beyond the two genders (male and female) that most people are most familiar with. Some trans people have non-binary identities, while others have more binary gender identities and identify as male/men or female/women.

A Note on Intersex

The particular Maddy who inspired this story is a person who has an intersex condition. The word intersex refers to a variety of conditions that lead to differences in development of physical sex characteristics. These conditions can involve differences in the external genitals, internal reproductive organs, sex chromosomes, or sex-related hormones. Conditions that result in genitals that blend characteristics of typical male genitals and typical female genitals tend to be identified at birth. Conditions that impact how puberty unfolds are often identified around puberty. Sometimes intersex conditions are identified later in life, for example because they impact fertility.

Intersex conditions are life-long conditions, and may be treated in a variety of ways depending on the needs of the person affected. Adults with intersex conditions have made recommendations based on their experience to help parents and doctors of children with intersex conditions understand what treatment is and is not needed. Where possible, decisions about possible treatment options should ideally be decided by the person with the intersex condition when they are old enough to do so.

Not all people who have intersex conditions identify as intersex. Most people who have intersex conditions identify with the gender they are assigned at birth. Some people who have intersex conditions have a binary gender identity that aligns with the other gender. Some people who have intersex conditions have non-binary gender identities—like the Maddy who inspired this story. In short, people who are born with intersex conditions may have a range of gender identities, just like people who are born without intersex conditions. This Note will discuss parents who are trans and gender diverse.

When a Parent Transitions

In some families a parent "comes out" as trans after the family has been formed and children are already included in the family. A parent's transition can be a challenging time for children, who may have feelings of grief for how their parent looked prior to coming out. Children may be unsure what their parent's transition means for their relationship with their parent. The children and family members of a transitioning parent are also going through a process of transition or transformation. It is a journey that can be highly emotional for the whole family, and can have various ups and downs. It can change the way a child sees the world. This story presents one way of understanding who the trans parent is and at the same time affirming that the parent is first and foremost a parent.

Emphasize that they are still the child's parent.

COLAGE's "Transition Tips for Parents" highlights the importance of parents letting their child know through words and actions that no matter what, they are still the child's parent. This is reflected in this story in that Maddy is actively engaged in parenting throughout. Ideally it helps if spouses and co-parents can present a united front and affirm that the transgender or gender diverse parent will continue to be the child's parent.

Find terms that are comfortable for you and your child.

Changes that affect day-to-day life during a parent's transition can include changes in the parent's pronouns, name, appearance, and overall gender expression. Children are faced with adjusting how they refer to their parent, which can take practice and may evolve over time. It's important not to rush children to give up familiar terms for a loving parent-child bond; it may be important for children to still call their parent "mommy" or "daddy" for their own comfort and consistency during the transition process. In the long run, a parent who transitions may no longer be comfortable with previous labels like "mommy" or "daddy," and the family may move away from them. Children and parents may choose a new title such as "Maddy" which blends mommy and daddy. Children may decide to change titles to those traditionally used for the new gender. Sometimes transition results in a family that now has two mothers or two fathers, and the whole family may be involved in deciding how they each want to be referred to. (For example, some families with two mothers use "Mama" and "Mommy," or "Mommy" in combination with their names.) This can be a way to honor the continued importance and uniqueness of the connection parents who are not transitioning have with their children. Sometimes the child will choose to use the parent's new first name or a nickname which might be a variation of the parent's previous name. Different children in the same family may have different preferences or move at different paces in adjusting to these changes. Using terms of affection and parental connection that feel right for your child and making changes at your child's pace are examples of how you can demonstrate the continued importance of your bond with your child.

When A Parent Is Already Living in Their Affirmed Gender

In other cases, transgender or gender diverse parents become parents after they are already living in their affirmed gender. In these cases, the children do not experience a change in who their parent is. Parents are faced with deciding what and how they will tell their children about their gender history. Some parents in these families may also identify as Maddies, Mapas, Babas, or other terms which reflect a parent's non-binary gender. Other parents in these families identify as Mommies and Daddies. In either case, it can be affirming for children to see families like theirs (such as in this book).

Discussing Gender Identity With Your Child

In all cases, it is importance to discuss parents' gender identities in an age-appropriate way focused on your child's needs. Use age-appropriate language, answer questions honestly and simply, and find any answers you don't yet know. Discussing details about gender affirming medical treatment may be overwhelming for young children who do not ask for more information in this area. In terms of timing of coming out, preschool-age children seem to adapt to their parent's transition best, then adult children, and adolescents often have the hardest time adjusting. There is evidence that delaying disclosure can have negative impacts on the parent-child relationship.

Navigating Bias

Children of trans parents may be faced with navigating anti-transgender bias and may experience minority stress due to anti-transgender discrimination. However, there are factors that protect against minority stress at the individual level, in relationships, in communities, and in society at large.

You can help your child be involved and empowered in choosing various strategies to navigate anti-transgender bias. For example, children may choose to be selective about who they tell about their parent being trans, or in how they refer to their trans parent in various situations. In other situations, they may prefer to speak up and affirm their experience of their family. It can be important for parents not to take these strategies personally.

Foster resilience.

Having a positive self-concept can include having a positive concept of who one's family is. Children can be supported in recognizing the gifts involved in having a transgender parent, such as an appreciation for "in-betweenness" (like in this story), or for the wide range of diversity in the world. Supportive family bonds are a powerful resiliency factor. This includes both trans parents and non-trans parents. A positive relationship between the parents themselves is another important protective factor.

Connect with supportive communities.

Participation in supportive communities is also an important factor when dealing with minority stress. Meeting other children from families with transgender parents or other families with transgender members can be normalizing and foster resilience. You can help your child to connect with such communities (such as COLAGE, which has some resources specifically for children of trans parents). Children of trans parents may choose to participate in Gay Straight Alliance (GSA) clubs. In participating in supportive communities, children can also become important resources for others. Being able to positively contribute also fosters resiliency.

Elicit the support of your child's school.

The school environment, including the reaction of teachers and parents of other children, will have a big effect on your child's experience, as this is a community in which they spend much of their time. If schools can be enlisted as supportive environments, they can become important sources of resiliency. On the other hand, dealing with social stigma at school (whether from teachers, peers, or the parents of peers) can lead to decline in school performance for the child of a trans parent. GLSEN found that when schools had policies supportive of trans students, such students were more likely to be engaged in school. Such policies may have similar protective effects for children of trans parents. Work with people in your child's life to elicit their support.

Seek professional supports.

Trans affirmative psychologists and other providers can be another source of support for trans people, their partners, and their families. Sometimes, a psychologist will best be able to support the child of a trans parent by working with the parents, at other times a psychologist might work directly with the child or with the whole family.

Resources

"Answers to Your Questions About Transgender People, Gender Identity, and Gender Expression"
American Psychological Association
www.apa.org/topics/lgbt/transgender

Intersex Information and Peer Support
Bodies Like Ours
Bodieslikeours.org

"Protecting the Rights of Transgender Parents and Their Children: A Guide for Parents and Lawyers"
American Civil Liberties Union
www.aclu.org/report/protecting-rights-transgender-parents-and-their-children

Resources for People With Trans Parents
COLAGE
www.colage.org/resources/people-with-trans-parents/

Resources for People with Transgender Family Members
Human Rights Campaign
www.hrc.org/resources/entry/resources-for-people-with-transgender-family-members

"FAQ About Transgender Parenting"
Lambda Legal
www.lambdalegal.org/know-your-rights/transgender/trans-parenting-faq

"Understanding Non-Binary People: How to Be Respectful and Supportive"
National Center for Transgender Equality transequality.org/issues/resources/understanding-non-binary-people-how-to-be-respectful-and-supportive

RANDALL D. EHRBAR, PSYD, *is a clinical psychologist who has focused on supporting trans people and their families throughout his career, for which he was named a Fellow of the American Psychological Association (APA). He participated in an APA task force on trans concerns—which among other things led to APA Resolution on Transgender, Gender Identity, and Gender Expression Nondiscrimination—as well as an APA task force charged with developing Guidelines for Psychological Practice With Transgender and Gender Nonconforming People. He has also been actively involved in the World Professional Association of Transgender Health (WPATH) and in revision of their Standards of Care for the health of trans people. He currently lives and works in the Washington, DC area and is proud to be called "Dad" by his children.*